OWL

PENGUIN

GULL

YEARBOOK

To all children with the courage to follow their dreams

ATHENEUM BOOKS FOR YOUNG READERS
An imprint of Simon & Schuster Children's Publishing Division
1230 Avenue of the Americas, New York, New York 10020

For information about special discounts for bulk purchases, please contact Simon & Schuster Special Sales at 1-866-506-1949 or business@simonandschuster.com.
The Simon & Schuster Speakers Bureau can bring authors to your live event. For more information or to book an event, contact the Simon & Schuster Speakers Bureau at 1-866-248-3049 or visit our website at www.simonspeakers.com.
Book design by Ann Bobco
The text for this book was set in Times New Roman MT Std.
The illustrations for this book were rendered in pencil and watercolor.
Manufactured in China
1018 SCP
First Edition
10 9 8 7 6 5 4 3 2 1
Library of Congress Cataloging-in-Publication Data
Names: Judge, Lita, author, illustrator.
Title: Penguin flies home / Lita Judge.
Description: First edition. | New York : Atheneum, [2019] | Series: Flight school | Summary: Even though his penguin friends would rather swim, Penguin dreams
of flying.
Identifiers: LCCN 2018003525 | ISBN 9781534414419 (hardcover) | ISBN 9781534414426 (eBook)
Subjects: | CYAC: Penguins—Fiction. | Flight—Fiction. | Individuality—Fiction.
Classification: LCC PZ7.J894 Pe 2019 | DDC [E]—dc23
LC record available at https://lccn.loc.gov/2018003525

LITA JUDGE

Penguin Flies Home

a Flight School story

Miss You xx
We Hope you are enjoying Flight School
To
xxx All the other penguins

Atheneum
Books for Young Readers
New York
London
Toronto
Sydney
New Delhi

Penguin loved to fly.

It was true he needed a little help with the technical parts—but that's why he worked hard as a student at flight school.

And as his teacher said, "It isn't feathers that you need most to fly. It's heart, and this penguin has heart."

"And the soul
of an eagle!"
Penguin
added.

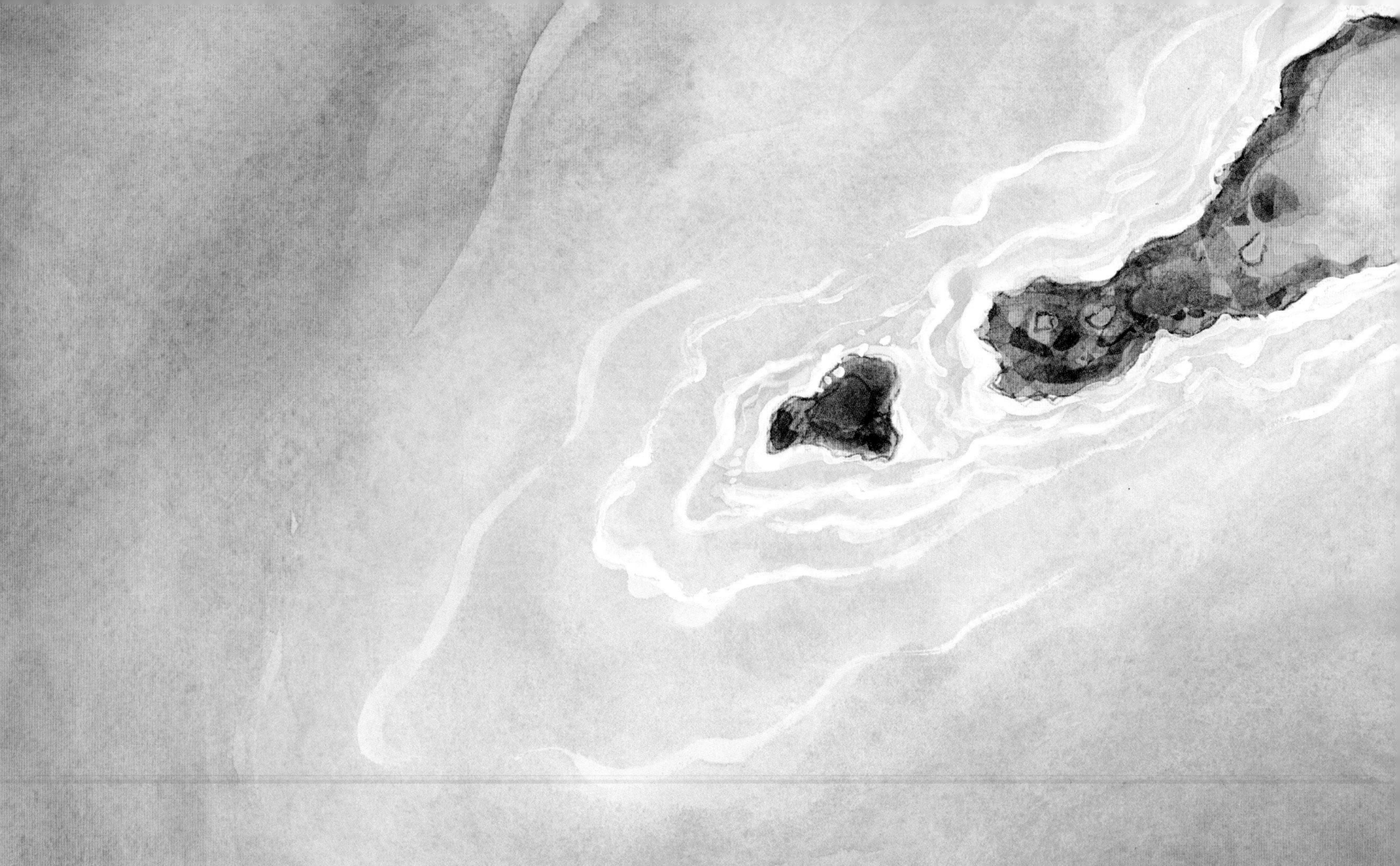

Penguin loved everything about flying:

the feel of the wind beneath his wings,
the song that rose from his little round belly,
the sight of new and wonderful places.

Everything except . . .

for that whisper of sadness that
drifted into his heart
when the sun set and the stars
floated overhead.

He knew his penguin friends, far away at home, were looking at those same stars.

"I wish they could feel the wind beneath their wings like I do," he told Teacher and Flamingo.

Penguin must be homesick, thought Teacher.

She and Flamingo thought all night,
and by dawn they had hatched a
beautiful plan.

At takeoff the next morning,
Teacher declared, “Field trip!”

Soon the birdies were flying

farther than they ever had before.

They flipped and flapped for days,
which turned into weeks,
until at last . . .

they had brought Penguin home.

Penguin's friends gathered the
moment he arrived.
They had missed him, too!

Penguin introduced them to Teacher, Flamingo, and Egret.
He told them all about his adventures at flight school,
and then he said Teacher could show them how to . . .

FLY!

"Follow me, birdies!"
Penguin said.
"It's time for class to begin."

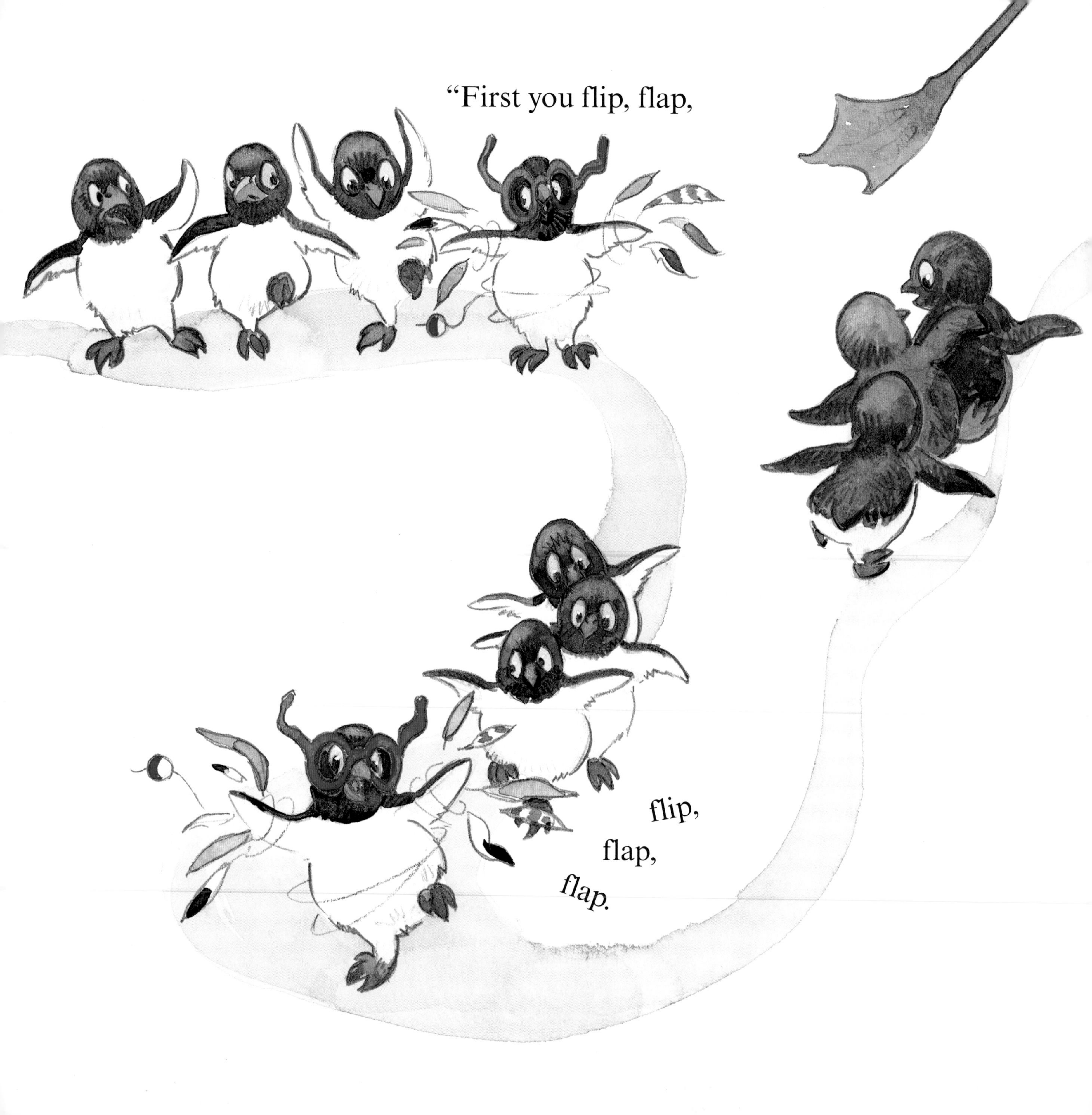

"First you flip, flap,

flip,
flap,
flap.

“And then
you
jump
up,

up,
up,
UP!

"Now, birdies,
before we can take off,
we must practice our landings!"

I think I'll go swim!
Yes!
Swimming!
Plop
Plop

We are penguins! We love to swim!

In their excitement they rushed off . . .

leaving Penguin alone.

“Why don’t they want to fly?” he asked Flamingo.

“Not everyone is like you, dear, with dreams as high as the stars.”

“They must think I’m ridiculous,” Penguin said.

He went to sit by himself.

Will my friends like me
if we don't share the same dreams?

As the sun sank,
the midnight sky began to shimmer,
and the desire to fly called out to him
from deep inside his soul.

You have to listen to things that deep,
even if it means you will be different
from everyone else.

The next morning Penguin walked slowly back
to tell his friends he was going to return with
Teacher, Flamingo, and Egret
to flight school.

But the colony was waiting for him with a . . .

OUR
FRIEND
PENGUIN
DREAMER
& FLYER
EXTRAORDINAIRE

The other penguins didn’t think he was ridiculous.

They were proud of him!

They told him they were sad to see him leave,
but they understood he had to
follow his dreams.

That no matter how far he flew,
they promised to look up at the sky
and think of him.

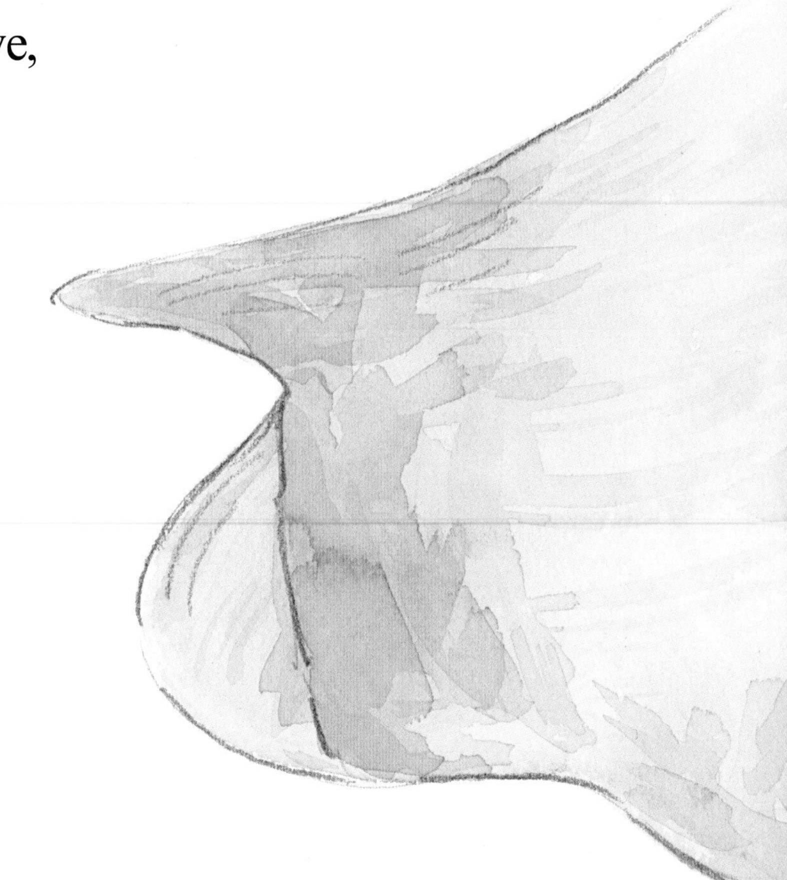

And that even if he had the soul of an eagle,
he would always be a little
round penguin, with dreams as high
as the stars . . .

and friends who love him.

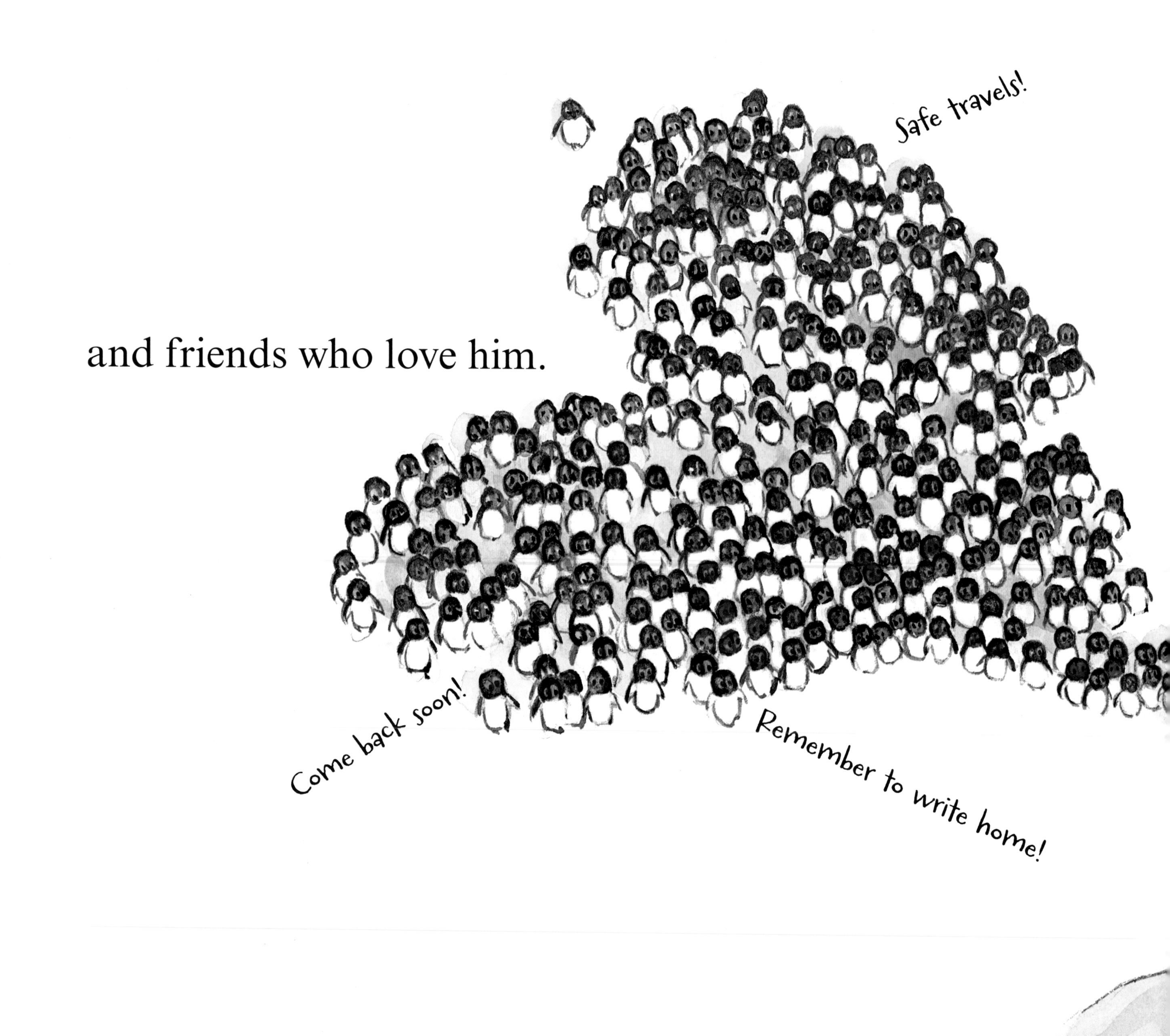

Safe travels!
Come back soon!
Remember to write home!

Penguin's Scrapbook

Best ice sculptor

BEST SWIMMER